VIRGINIA HAMILTON

BRUH RABBIT

and the

TAR BABY GIRL

paintings by James E. Ransome

THE BLUE SKY PRESS

An Imprint of Scholastic Inc. • New York

THE BLUE SKY PRESS

Library of Congress catalog card number: 2002015529

ISBN 0-590-47376-X

10 9 8 7 6 5 4 3 2 1   03 04 05 06 07

Printed in Singapore   46

First printing, October 2003

Handlettering by David Coulson

Designed by Kathleen Westray

FOR
VIRGINIA
HAMILTON
—J.R.

It was a far time ago, and before a first winter snow, that Bruh Wolf had a run-in with pesty Bruh Rabbit. Bruh Wolf planted corn one year, and Bruh Rabbit didn't plant a thing. Rabbit, him, is tricky-some—about to fool a body and not do a lick of work himself.

All winter long, Bruh Rabbit lived on Wolf's corn. He stole as much as he could eat. The next year, Bruh Wolf planted peanuts. Bruh Rabbit did him the same way. He ate all he could of Wolf's store and planted nary a thing himself.

Now Bruh Wolf was thinking something be not quite right. One day, he went out to look over his peanut patch, and he looked hard at the rabbit tracks. Said, "Guess me, somebody been into my peanuts."

It happened again, next day. Rabbit tracks. Shells all about. "For true, somebody been here, eating up everything," Wolf says. So he makes him a scarey-crow and sets it up in the middle of the peanut patch.

Daylean passes, night comes, and so does the moon and Bruh Rabbit. Rabbit sneakity-sneaks along. He's got his croker sack to carry the peanuts. He's creeping low-down, slow-down, and he sees the scarey-crow—WHOOM!—standing still and very white in the shine of the moon.

"What's that?" Bruh Rabbit saying. Nobody else says a thing.

"I say, who's that?" Bruh Rabbit speaks louder. And nobody says a thing one more time. Rabbit hasn't seen nobody move, either.

So he sidles closer and a little closer until he's real close to what-it-was in the peanut patch. Way slow, Bruh Rabbit lifts his paw to touch the what-it-was.

Jump back! Says, "You are a bundle of old rags! Fool, Wolf, if he thinks this rabbit is afraid of you!"

Bruh Rabbit kicked over the scarey-crow. He filled his sack with peanuts, cracked a few open and ate them, and scurried home to his place in the briar bush.

Dayclean comes in, and Wolf sees somebody has been at his peanuts again. Shells all around. And there's his scarey-crow, all knocked down and torn up.

Bruh Wolf's so mad his fur climbs his neck! He can't stand it. "I'll fix that old rabbit. Just wait till I show him a thing or two!"

Wolf takes out his coal-tar bucket. It's about half full of the blackest, shiniest tar you ever did see. He sets himself down and gets ready. "I'm-a make me one baby girl rabbit outta tar and set her in the peanut patch. Just let old Bruh Rabbit try to knock over my tar baby girl, and we'll see!"

By 'n by, daylean ends, and night begins. The rabbit comes with his croker sack over his shoulder. And who does he see?

Tar Baby Girl, that's who, standing black in the moonshine.

"What's that?" Rabbit says. "Old Wolf set him up another scarey-crow?" He moves himself closer, looking harder, 'n says, "This can't be another scarey-crow. This seems like a little girl. I best study upon this here."

Bruh Rabbit spreads out his sack and sits down in the middle of the peanut patch. He's staring at the tar baby. At last he speaks to her. "Girl, what they name you?"

Girl won't say anything.

"Girl, why won't you speak to me? What you doing out here?"

Bruh Rabbit listens for a while. All he hears is the whippoorwill in the swamp.

He scoots closer. "Girl! Speak to me! If you don't, I'll knock you. Knock you with my right paw, and you'll think it's thunder!"

Tar Baby Girl can't say a thing. Bruh Rabbit takes a swing at her with his right paw—BLAM! His paw gets stuck!

Oh, that rabbit can holler! "Girl, lemme go! Why do you hold me so? If you don't lemme go, I'll knock you silly with my left paw. You'll think it's thunder and lightning together."

Tar Baby Girl won't let him go. He swings at her. FAPOOM! His left paw's stuck! "Girl, let me loose, else I'll right-foot kick you, and you'll think it be a cow kicking you!"

Tar Baby Girl doesn't move.

You know what happens now: PLICK! Right foot is good 'n stuck. BLICK! Horse-kick, and left foot is way stuck, too.

"I haven't done a thing to you, Missy Girl," says the rabbit. "Turn me loose, and I won't meddle with you. You think I can't do nothing? I can still bite, and it'll be worse than a snake bite."

Missy Girl, keeping her mouth shut. Bruh Rabbit took a bite. GUNK! His nose stuck! He sure was one rabbit stuck on somebody!

Before sun-up it was, Wolf came over to the peanut patch. And there he found Bruh Rabbit.

"Hee-hee!" he hollered. "You a stuck-up bruh, for true! Bruh, you been a thief in my corn and my peanuts. And now, I'm-a going to eat you!"

He pulled the rabbit out of the tar baby girl.

"Oh, Bruh Wolf, don't do me so, I beg you," Bruh Rabbit cried. "You may roast me and toast me; you may cut me up and eat me. But whatever you do, *don't throw me in the briar bush!*"

"Huh? You don't want me to throw you in the briars—
that's just what I'm-a do!" Bruh Wolf grabbed Bruh
Rabbit by his ears and flung him into the deepest,
thickest, briarest bush you ever saw.

Bruh Rabbit disappeared in there. But Wolf could hear him laughing. "Oh! Oh! Split my sides! Oh!" hollers the rabbit. "My whole family was born in here. I was born and bred here! Wolf, you so foolish. You'll never catch me again!" And with that, the rabbit went on his way.

Watch out behind you, Bruh Wolf! Better look out for Bruh Rabbit when next the day leans over and night falls down.

ABOUT THIS STORY

Bruh Rabbit, also known as B'rabby, Brer Rabbit, or Buh Rabbit, was the favorite animal character of Plantation Era storytellers in the South. The early generations of African American tellers during slavery knew that the little rabbit they saw hopping along was small and helpless compared to other animals, such as the bear, wolf, and fox. They were helpless as well, and they began to identify the rabbit's lowly status with their own. And yet, Bruh Rabbit was smart and could get himself out of almost any jam. He was tricky and clever, usually winning over the wolf and bear.

In *Bruh Rabbit and the Tar Baby Girl*, this trickiest of tricksters takes on Wolf. Bruh Rabbit is caught in the act of thievery; but by his escape skills, he gets away yet again. *Bruh*

Rabbit and the Tar Baby Girl is one version of the classic tar baby story, of which there are hundreds of versions. This one stands out because Wolf makes a "scarey-crow" first before fashioning the tar baby girl. In the very earliest versions of this tale, the tar baby is described as a girl.

A croker sack, also spelled croaker and crocker, is a burlap bag. It is also called a crocus sack and can be a sack in which small croaking animals, such as frogs, are kept. Generally, the old-fashioned word is thought to mean a burlap bag in which food and other things are carried.

Dayclean and daylean refer to dawn (dayclean) when the day begins and evening (daylean) when the sun slants westward, going down.

This version of the story was collected and recorded in fairly heavy Gullah speech of the Sea Islands of South Carolina.